A NANNY FOR THE PROFESSOR

CASS KINCAID

Copyright © Cass Kincaid 2024

All rights reserved.

No part of this book may be reproduced in any form or by any electronic or mechanical means, including information storage and retrieval systems, without written permission from the author and publisher, except for the use of brief quotations embodied in critical articles and book reviews.

This is a work of fiction.

ISBN: 979-8-3304-1519-9

Cover image: Adobestock

Published in the United States of America by EverLust Books an imprint of Harbor Lane Books, LLC.

www.everlustbooks.com

CHAPTER
ONE
BROCK

"You can't be serious." Brock was exhausted. Sleep had never sounded so good. And yet, here he was listening to Anna, the woman he'd depended on and relied on for the past six months to look after his daughter while he worked, tell him that she was taking another job. Her dream job.

Like getting to hang out with his four-year-old daughter, Rynn, wasn't a dream job of its own.

Hell, it was *his* dream job. But getting to stay home and color in coloring books while eating macaroni and cheese and hiding out in blanket forts in the living room didn't pay the bills.

Which was exactly why he'd hired Anna, a nanny through the local agency, so he could take on the full-time professor position at Grexton University and provide everything he could to Rynn. And everything had been going well, completely according to plan.

Until now.

"I'm sorry, Mr. Hanlin. I just can't turn down—"

"Anna, you haven't called me Mr. Hanlin in months. There's no need to now."

"No," she agreed. "But you sound mad. And when you sound mad, I get super professional. Call it a defense mechanism."

Brock could relate to that. Hell knows he had a few of his own defense mechanisms he tended to refer to when the situation called for it. "I'm not mad," he insisted, running a hand through his dirty blond hair. "Just disappointed. Not in you, of course, just the situation as a whole." As much as he wanted to, he couldn't blame her for taking the preschool job in Calledon. She was overqualified to be here babysitting every day—he knew that. But he'd thought he found the perfect companion for Rynn while he worked. And his daughter loved the woman, jabbered on about their activities and days spent doing outings and fun things. "You got along with Rynn so well."

"I know." Anna sighed, pushing her dark brown hair past her shoulder. "And I'm sad to leave her. But I couldn't turn down the opportunity, *Brock*."

"I get it. I really do." He checked the calendar on his cellphone, then eyed her hopefully. "And there's no way you can give me more notice?" It was a long shot, but he had to ask.

"The job starts on Monday," she replied sadly. "I'm really sorry."

"Don't be." He pushed the phone into his pocket. "I'll figure it out." *I always do*, he thought. "Congrats on the new job, Anna. I really do wish you the best."

To his surprise, Anna leaned forward and hugged Brock before she thanked him and disappeared out the door.

Six months, and now he was starting all over again. Damn it. He didn't relish the thought of telling Rynn when she woke up in the morning. In that moment, a sliver of frustration jolted through him at knowing Anna hadn't had the guts to tell the little girl herself.

Oh well, he would be the one to break the bad news. To hold his little daughter as she cried big tears from her sparkly blue eyes that reminded him so much of her mama's.

Not for the first time, Brock wished Hailey, Rynn's mom, was there. But fate had thrown a wrench into their plans for a lifetime together three years ago when Hailey was in a car accident that left the Hanlins as a family of two.

Brock shook his head. He couldn't think about that. He had to do what was best for his daughter, like he always did. And that meant getting on the phone with the nanny agency and finding a suitable replacement for Rynn's caretaker.

By Monday.

He groaned. It was a Friday night. He'd just got home from teaching a three-hour lecture on the prose of Hemingway. The agency wouldn't be open now, but there was a number for one of the managers he could call tomorrow morning since he was in a pinch.

He would make it right, do whatever he had to do. For Rynn.

Saturday morning was a time for cartoons and pajamas in the Hanlin household. Rynn, even at four years old, always seemed to sleep in a little later, which was the biggest gift Brock could ever receive seeing as he was a single dad with a full-time job and very little spare time.

But Saturday mornings, those were reserved for daddy and daughter time.

Usually, anyway.

"Your cereal is getting soggy, Rynn Tin Tin."

Rynn came flying out of the living room, her little bare feet padding loudly across the laminate floor and the area run, and she pushed her cereal bowl up on the kitchen table, milk sloshing over the side onto the tabletop. "I'm all done!" she announced before racing back to her favorite spot in front of the television, eyes wide as she watched colorfully-clothed puppies bounce around on the screen, saving their kitten friends from some kind of peril.

Ah, cartoons. If only every daunting situation could be solved within a half-hour timespan, with everyone happy and content again by the time the credits rolled.

Fortunately, just the sight of Rynn sitting cross-legged on the floor in her *101 Dalmations* pajamas and her long chestnut hair in a curly mess seemed to put Brock at ease. She always seemed to be the one to help him get through the tough things, and the little girl didn't even know she was doing it. He would do absolutely anything for a simple "Daddy, I love you," though—that's what made his world revolve.

And now, clad in his own red plaid pajama pants and plain white T-shirt, Brock had to pull himself away from those cartoons and that porcelain doll he called a daughter and handle something he didn't want to have to be handling. It couldn't be helped.

"Daddy's just going to make a phone call, baby girl." He picked his cellphone up off the kitchen table. "I'll just be in the kitchen."

He hadn't been able to bring himself to tell her about Anna's departure as her nanny yet. He needed a pot of coffee and a chance to steel himself against her impending breakdown before he announced the news.

Brock also figured it'd be better to have someone lined up to tell Rynn about before he tried to explain. He dialed the manager's number and let it ring, already feeling guilty for making a business call on a Saturday morning. But the business in question was his daughter's care, so good luck telling him it wasn't a good time.

"I'm sorry to call so early on a weekend," he said when the thick-voiced manager answered on the other end. "It's Brock Hanlin."

Immediately, the manager perked up—he'd heard the

news that Anna's notice had been given. For all the notice it was. She was gone, with no time to ease into the transition.

"No need to worry, Mr. Hanlin," the manager assured him in the most theatrically encouraging voice Brock had ever heard. "I've got a new hire that would be perfect to step in and take Anna's place. Your little Rynn will love her, and I'm sure you will, too."

Doubtful I'd go that far. "As long as she's here by Monday morning so I can meet her and observe her with Rynn before I have to teach my afternoon class, that sounds good. Thank you."

All he could hope was that Rynn *did* love her, because Brock was out of options.

CHAPTER TWO

CAMILLA

She was hesitant, right from the get-go. After all, Camilla had just gotten out of the most nightmarish nanny position she'd ever experienced in her life. It was also the only job as a nanny she'd ever had, so she didn't have anything else to compare it to. But if that was what being a nanny was all about—dealing with two six-year-old twin boys who had a fondness for setting makeshift traps that inflicted pain on their unwitting victims and purposely destroying things in their parents' home just so the babysitter would get in trouble, Camilla wanted no part of this career choice anymore.

Unfortunately, she had no other prospects at the moment, and the nanny agency's call came before she had the chance to win the lottery and run off to some beautiful tropical island.

Another nanny position. This time, caring for a four-year-old girl. The agency manager swore she was a delight to be with, and that the parents were reasonable and excellent clients who'd just been left hanging by their previous nanny, who'd taken another job and left them without help.

Camilla felt bad enough about that, which was why she

accepted the position despite getting a call on a Saturday morning about it, and despite being ridiculously skeptical that the little girl was an angel—the manager's words, not hers—and the parents were as easy to get along with as she was led to believe.

Either way, Camilla was twenty-one years old, with an apartment to pay for and other bills to pay. She needed a job. So, she agreed to meet with the father of the little girl on Monday morning and let him interview her—he'd probably interrogate her, that was more accurate—while she met her new client and then stayed for the afternoon.

Which led her there, to the cobblestone front step she stood on, where she knocked on the front door and gaped at the old-world charm of the estate-like home before her. It wasn't massive, but the elegance the building portrayed, the intricate stonework and wrought irons railings, made the house more beautiful and fancy in her eyes than any oversized mansion ever could.

The door swung open, and if Camilla's mouth wasn't hanging open at the sight of the house, it was now, due to the sight of the man standing in front of her.

He was older than she was, maybe mid or late thirties. He wore a crisp white dress shirt, buttoned all the way up except for the top button or two, and his hair was gelled to give it that styled-yet-messy look she'd seen only perfected in commercials. A dark shadow of stubble lined his cheeks, chin, and upper lips, but it was neat and tidy and…intoxicating. Paired with his eyes, a sheer blue that pierced through her and made it impossible to look away, and his obviously chiseled body beneath the otherwise muted shirt and khakis, Camilla wasn't sure she'd ever seen a more alluring man in her entire life.

"Oh, wow…hey, I mean. You must be Camilla Benton….right?"

He sounded just as unsure as she felt. That was when

Camilla realized she was staring at him, wide-eyed. The only saving grace was that he looked caught off guard, too.

"Yeah." She shook her head, trying to clear her racing thoughts. She held a hand out in an attempt to prove she had some manners. "I'm Camilla. The agency called me this weekend about your nanny leaving your family on short notice. I apologize for that inconvenience, by the way."

"I'm Brock, Rynn's dad." He shook her hand, and Camilla wasn't sure if he could feel the heat that seeped between their touching skin. It seemed to set her ablaze deep inside, far past the point where only their fingers touched, making her cheeks heat up in response. "Come in, Camilla. Rynn's just in the living room."

She followed him inside, glancing down at her gray linen pants and dark purple long-sleeved shirt, wondering idly if she looked okay. Then, she wondered why she cared.

Oh, right, because your new boss is sexy as hell.

She shook the thought from her mind—she didn't need that kind of distraction, especially not today when she was supposed to be making a good first impression. She was bound to make a fool of herself if she didn't focus on what mattered most—Rynn, the little girl her world would revolve around each day.

"Rynn, there's somebody here to meet you."

Camilla noticed how Brock's voice changed when he called out to his daughter. An octave higher, softer, more affectionate. It was downright adorable.

"Just a heads-up," Brock added, almost wincing. "She only found out Anna wasn't coming back last night. I can't decide if she's okay about the whole thing yet or not."

There was no time to feel out the situation. The little girl came sprinting out of the living room, where, through the open-concept living room, Camilla could see a cartoon on the television screen with bouncing alphabet letters bobbing across it.

The first thing she noticed was the girl's eyes—piercing and gorgeous, just like her father's. But they had a different shape, more almond than round. Her hair was slightly lighter than Brock's, and it trailed down her back in loose, buoyant curls. She looked like one of the fancy dolls Camilla's mom used to collect in a china cabinet in their living room when she was growing up.

"Well, hey, Rynn." Camilla bent forward, hands on her hips. "It's good to finally meet you."

The little girl stopped an arm's length from her, eyeing her up conspicuously. "You don't look like Anna."

Not off to a good start, she thought, but she kept a smile plastered on her face. "Maybe not, but I bet we'll have lots of fun, anyway."

"What's your name?" For a four-year-old, Rynn was quick. Maybe the interrogation wasn't going to come from her father after all.

"Camilla."

"Like the puppy stealer?" Rynn screeched out the words, her eyes wide to show how appalled she was.

"What? No!" Camilla could barely keep her expression neutral, biting back her laughter. "Camilla, not Cruella. Rynn, I love puppies, but I promise I don't steal them."

The little girl slowly narrowed her eyes, mulling it over. Finally, she nodded as though she'd come to some sort of conclusion. "Okay, then. You can come and watch *101 Dalmatians* with me." The little girl reached out for her hand and tugged her toward the living room, her mind made up.

Camilla glanced up at Brock. It was her turn for her eyes to be wide. But Brock didn't look alarmed at all. In fact, the corners of his mouth had curled up and he was pressing his lips together, amused.

"Looks like you've passed the test," he joked, mumbling to her as his daughter pulled her past him.

"I have a funny feeling I'm going to be owned by this little girl before the day's done," she chuckled under her breath.

She couldn't be sure because Rynn was pulling her away from him, but Camilla thought she heard him mutter, "Welcome to the club."

CHAPTER
THREE
BROCK

Whatever Brock expected when he opened that door, Camilla Benton wasn't it. Her eyes were chocolate and dark-lashed, and her hair was such a rich shade of auburn that he hadn't known such a color existed. The slender frame of her body dressed in casual linen-blend pants and a deep purple shirt was thin, but her outfit was fitted enough to show the shapeliness of her arms and thighs. The woman was athletic, maybe a runner or a fan of yoga.

And she was sexy as sin. Naturally beautiful, her eyes held the hint of makeup—maybe mascara, but he didn't know one pencil or tube of the stuff from the next—but it wasn't needed. Camilla exuded beauty in a quiet way.

But it was a very, very real way, and it had Brock's body humming with the appreciation of it.

Then, he had watched Rynn assess the woman with the narrowed eyes of a seasoned negotiator, like she had a mental checklist she was checking off as her eyes roamed up the woman and then back down to her sock-covered toes in the kitchen. Whatever his daughter saw in Camilla Benton, she liked it.

So did Brock. And that worried him a bit. At least, it did until he spent the rest of the morning grading essays at the kitchen table, coffee cup cradled beside him, listening to the woman and child discussing the television show that was on but they were only half-watching, Camilla prompting Rynn to count along with the cartoon characters and Rynn proudly proving that she could. They wound up in a magical, make-believe world of their own, transforming into Princess Rynn and Queen Cam—as Rynn quickly shortened her name to—and Brock actually felt bad for having to interrupt them when he pulled his briefcase into his hand and headed for the door to teach his evening class.

"Everything good here?" he asked, amused at seeing Camilla with a plastic tiara on her head, one that matched Rynn's to a tee.

"Everything is wonderful," Camilla chuckled, standing to her full height. "Time for work?"

"I've got a three-hour lecture until ten o'clock," he explained. "There's a list on the fridge of the approximate times and activities Rynn is used to in the evenings. If you have any questions, my cellphone number is on it, too." His eyes met hers. "Use it any time, Queen Cam."

It could have been the trick of the light, but he thought he saw Camilla's cheeks redden. And he might have known for sure if he hadn't been so enamored by the way her eyes darkened when he spoke.

She heard the innuendo in his voice, the promise.

He kissed her daughter on the forehead and told her he loved her, then strode out the front door, fully aware that Camilla wasn't the only one whose body was coming alive at that very same unspoken promise.

After Monday's late afternoon lecture, Brock broke a few speed limits wanting to get home. He couldn't wait to hear about the evening Rynn and Camilla had enjoyed together, but he wanted to hear it from the nanny's mouth. That way, the next morning he could compare her story with Rynn's own version.

He could always count on his daughter to be brutally honest, and while he might have liked the way Camilla interacted with Rynn, seeming to hit it off straight away, the real test came after he was no longer in the vicinity. Rynn would be sure to spell it out for him whether Camilla was someone Rynn liked to be around.

God, Brock hoped she did. Not just because she seemed the perfect match for Rynn's level of excitement and energy, but because he couldn't quite put a finger on his own immediate reaction to the woman. The mere sight of her had done something to him, making him race home and want to see, not only Rynn as usual, but Camilla as well. It was a foreign feeling he didn't quite understand after three years of avoiding anything of the romantic sort.

Not that this was anything of that sort, he told himself.

Not yet, anyway.

He unlocked the front door and slipped inside. Silence welcomed him. The television was in darkness, no light at all coming from the living room. The kitchen had only the dim light above the oven on to guide his way as he passed through and down the hallway. Another golden stream of soft light cascaded out onto the wooden hallway floor.

It was late, well past ten-thirty, so Brock had expected Rynn to be fast asleep.

He hadn't expected to see Camilla curled up on the bed with his daughter, laying on top of the covers while Rynn snuggled in underneath, one arm slipped over Rynn's little body protectively. Both sleeping forms looked about as comfortable and peaceful as a person could.

Brock's heart squeezed tightly at the sight. Something was happening, something different. Rynn had loved Anna, but never in the six months of Anna being her nanny had the woman snuggled into bed with her until she fell asleep, a small pile of children's books scattered at the foot of the bed. Anna had been all business.

Camilla was different. This was her job, but she was about more than just the business of it. Camilla wasn't just all business—she was all Camilla. And he had a funny feeling his daughter was quickly becoming smitten by her.

Maybe she wasn't the only one.

CHAPTER **FOUR**
CAMILLA

The next morning, in the comfort of her own home, Camilla nursed a large mug of coffee while thinking back on the night before.

When she had awoken to Brock's lightly prodding fingers on her shoulder, she'd been mortified at having fallen asleep before he'd made it home from the university. The hours of building pretend castles with blankets and trying to help Rynn name all one hundred and one of the dalmatians in the movie just because the little girl told her to must have been more tiring than she realized.

But Brock had been anything but upset with her for falling asleep on the job. He had actually thanked her, and something told Camilla that his gratitude wasn't just from her staying with his daughter for the evening.

Hell, she felt like she should thank *him*. If last evening was any indication of what it was like to be the nanny of a child who wasn't in the running for the devil's most malicious spawn, then she was going to hold on to this job for dear life. The hours she spent with Rynn hadn't seemed like working. It didn't seem like a job to hang out with the little girl and play with dolls and dress-up clothes and wait for her daddy to come home. The truth was, for those few brief hours, they'd seemed very much like...

A family.

Camilla shook that thought away immediately. Brock Hanlin was her boss, nothing more. Rynn was the little girl she cared for in his absence. She needed to remember that, and she couldn't get too comfortable.

But it was hard. Because there was something about the way Brock stared at her, the way there always seemed to be a simmering quality to his gaze, like a fire burned somewhere in their deepest depths, just waiting to ignite into a blazing inferno.

And there was something about him that made Camilla sure that, if that was true, she would let him. Let the fire lick and lap at her sensitive flesh until it engulfed her completely, consuming her whole and reducing her resolve to ashes and embers.

She wanted Brock to spread through her like wildfire, and if the barely-contained blaze in his eyes was any indication, Brock wanted the same sinful flames to sear through him, too.

———

The next two days came and went in a flurry of coming and going. Brock taught two classes on Tuesdays, leaving Camilla with Rynn for the bulk of the day, and one long lecture on Wednesday mornings, but he had asked her to stay for a few more hours after he made it home Wednesday afternoon so he could keep his class curriculums and paper grading at bay. Judging by the stacks of essays he pulled from his briefcase, she didn't think it would be hard to end up behind in his paperwork if he left it for more than a few days.

She might have only seen him in passing, and not for more than a few minutes at a time during the day, but when Brock did finally come home from work, they seemed to linger around each other. Camilla couldn't seem to make herself leave, and Brock always seemed to be a step away, asking questions and keeping the conversation going to make her stay.

She could almost hear the buzzing in the air between them, the electricity and tension that crackled as they spoke and got close to one another but never touched. Their words might have held her there, giving her a reason to postpone having to walk out that door, but Camilla yearned to reach out and lay her fingertips along the bulging muscles of his biceps.

She could imagine the intensity in the stare that would follow, visualize the way his lips would part, hear the faint intake of breath that would break through the thick veil of sensual tension and bring them together, like a wall that had been built between them had been destroyed, causing them to crash together with the force of their unspoken desires.

There were more than enough reasons why they should deny the connection between them. He was her employer, after all, not to mention at least ten—maybe even fifteen or more—years older than she was. It would be wrong to pursue something between them, no matter what kind of tingles and heat the man was eliciting within her with just his gaze.

Thursday night, however, Camilla could tell that something had shifted between them the moment she arrived at Brock's place. He only had an evening class to teach that night, so it was already after six o'clock. Rynn would be getting ready for bed in an hour or so, and it would be a quiet night in the Hanlin household. An easy shift, if Camilla thought about it like a job. Which she didn't.

"Rynn Tin Tin can barely keep her eyes open as it is," Brock advised her when she joined him in the kitchen, watching him lock up the metal clasps on his briefcase. "She's got a pile of new books she can't wait to show you, but I doubt you'll make it through the first page of the first one and she'll be out like a light."

Camilla's stomach fluttered with the affectionate way Brock spoke of his daughter. She really was his world, and he didn't try to hide that for anyone. "I'll do my best to keep that in mind," she said, reaching across the kitchen counter to put her phone in the middle of it where she always kept it, so it wouldn't get broken during her and Rynn's playful antics, but also so she would know where it was.

At the same moment, Brock turned, reaching in the opposite direction for his car keys. Their hands collided, and they'd both leaned in, bringing their upper bodies and faces closer to each other than they'd ever been before.

Camilla could feel his warm, damp breath against her lips, and her eyes searched his as they both held perfectly still, transfixed by their sudden closeness and lost in the electricity that sparked between them and robbed them both of breath.

"I want you to keep something else in mind, too." Brock's voice was low, with a huskiness to it that hadn't been there a moment ago.

"Anything," she breathed out. Neither of them moved away from the other, but neither of them leaned in closer, either.

Brock's hot gaze was locked on her lips. "I want you to stay," he said. His gaze lifted to hers. "Tonight, after class, I want you to stay."

"You want me to...stay after class."

That made his mouth twitch at the corners. "Precisely. I'm glad I'm understood." Brock grabbed his briefcase and left without another word, leaving Camilla with only her shallow breaths and her racing heart to keep her company.

I want you to stay. Those five little words catapulted through Camilla's mind for hours, wondering if she was truly interpreting them the way he intended them.

Did he mean he wanted her to stay, as in stay the night? With him? In his bed?

Hell, that's how she hoped he meant it.

But there was a chance he meant he wanted her to stay for other reasons, too. Maybe she had done something he didn't approve of, or Rynn had said something to him that had him questioning her abilities as a caregiver. Camilla couldn't think of anything she could have done that would be misconstrued, but that didn't mean that a four-year-old couldn't see things differently.

Maybe Brock wasn't happy with her as Rynn's nanny. Maybe she just wasn't cut out for this kind of job. Hell, maybe he was going to fire her because of the sexual tension between them. If he felt it with the same insatiable desire she did, then there was a chance Brock Hanlin didn't want that kind of distraction, especially not when that distraction was supposed to be the one looking after the little girl that was his whole world.

That's it. Brock was going to dismiss her from his employ. It made the most sense. If he had truly intended for her to stay the night with him, to feel the rush of giving themselves over to the relentless need that pulsed between them like a lifeline, then surely he would have given her something more to cling to before he left. More words. More explanation.

Hell, he could have leaned in the mere inches between them and pressed his mouth to hers. That one little gesture would have told her everything she needed to know.

Instead, she was sprawled out on the couch in the living room after cleaning up the kitchen and snack dishes, wishing Rynn was awake just so she would have a distraction of her own to keep her rampant thoughts at bay. Wishing she knew something, anything, beyond the tidbit of information he'd given her.

She heard the door open and the beeping of the alarm being reset. In a way, it seemed like forever since Brock had left, and only minutes at the same time. Camilla let out a loud, steadying breath and stood, rounding the corner.

What met her on the other side of the wall answered every question without so much as a word uttered.

CHAPTER
FIVE
BROCK

In his nine-year history of being a university professor, Brock had never taught a class on autopilot.

Until tonight.

As he pulled the car into the driveway, he couldn't even recall what exactly he'd lectured on, or how well the students had received his lecture. That had never happened before. Brock took his career seriously, and he prided himself on being a good and well-liked teacher among the faculty at Grexton.

But tonight, something was more urgent. More dire and consuming.

And that something was Camilla Benton.

He'd asked her to stay on a whim, thinking she would turn him down in an instant. Despite their age difference, someone had to be the responsible one. It wasn't him, or he would have been able to refrain from asking her to stay in the first place, but it obviously wasn't going to be her, either.

Camilla wanted him. There was no way to hide the yearning that shrouded her eyes. He recognized it because he was sure he was wearing the same blatant need on his own face. He wanted her, too. With the heated desire of a thousand red-hot suns.

And his three-hour lecture had been governed by that desire, his need pulsing through him and growing with each minute that passed without her near him. Without her against him. Under him.

By the time he pressed the code into the front door of his house and stepped inside, all Brock's self-control had been swept away by the incessant throbbing of his hardness and the boiling of the blood in his veins. His resolve hung by a thread.

So, when Camilla came around the corner, eyes wide and fearful, there was nothing he could do but pull her to him in a frenzied hurry, desperate to feel her slender body against his in any way he could get it.

His mouth crashed down on hers as he pushed her up against the wall beside the doorway and pressed his entire body against her, fueled by the realization of just how perfectly she fit against him. He tasted her mouth hungrily, his tongue exploring every warm, wet inch of hers, tasting the sweetness that was all Camilla. She moaned against him, the decadent sound reverberating against his lips, only enticing him to continue, to take what he needed.

"Rynn..." He breathed out his daughter's name in a husky pant. "Tell me she's asleep."

"Yes." Camilla's own breath came out labored, in a rush. "For hours."

Relief washed over him as he pressed his forehead to hers, letting his tongue flick out to touch her bottom lip. The action, and the whimper it elicited from her throat, only made his rigid cock ache more brutally. "Stay with me."

"Are you sure that's a good idea?" she asked, but whether or not she realized it, Camilla was nodding while she spoke. Her fingertips had pulled the back of his dress shirt up, tracing sensual circles against his lower back.

Her body was betraying her even if her mind was holding on to some semblance of control.

"I frankly don't give a damn, Camilla." His eyes burned into hers. "I won't be gentle with you—I can't. I want you so goddamn bad I can barely think straight."

Brock wasn't sure he got the words out in full, wasn't sure who kissed who. But suddenly their mouths were colliding again, and this time Camilla's tongue tangled with his in a delicious dance that made every nerve ending within him spark with electricity. His hands were in her hair, his chest, abdomen, and pelvis crushed against hers, overcome by the unquenchable need to be closer to her, to be inside her.

His pulse pounded in his ears. Mixed with the moans and whimpers coming from Camilla, the sounds that surrounded him were driving him crazy, tugging at that last shred of control that held him back from dominating her in every dark and decadent way he could fathom.

Then, he felt her grind forward, pressing that soft, sweet spot at the apex of her thighs against his hardness in blissful agony, and everything inside Brock snapped.

A low growl escaped his throat as he reached behind her, cupping her ass and lifting her. No demand was needed for Camilla to wrap her legs around him and let him take her wherever he wanted.

She was his. His to do with what he wanted. What he *craved*.

Their kiss continued the entire way to the bedroom, and it took every ounce of strength Brock had not to slam the bedroom door shut and rip her clothes from her body like an animal. But he couldn't take a chance at waking Rynn, and he shifted Camilla to one arm as he slowly closed the door, listening for the click as he locked it behind him.

It was the only gentle thing he did. After that, there was nothing left to hold him back from devouring the woman before him like the sexy woman she was. He wanted to taste every inch of her, feel every inch of her creamy skin.

"Fuck, Cam—"

"Shh," she whispered. "*Show me.*"

Whatever resolve he had left dissipated in a cloud of smoke. In a tangle of limbs and frenzied kisses and touches, their clothes were peeled away, her fumbling with the buttons of his shirt and the buckle of his belt, him tugging at the hem of her shirt and the fly of her jeans. Layer by layer, skin was bared, areas that he kissed and licked because he had to, because he needed to feel the warmth of her flesh and the heat of her skin against his.

Camilla grazed her fingernails down his hard, chiseled chest, dragging a moan from his lips and a flinch of his muscles. Everything was so clenched, so constricted and tight and aching.

He let out a gruff sound of approval at the sight of her mauve lace bra and panties, pushing her back onto the plush comforter of his bed so he could take in the full view, from her long legs to the visible beat of her pulse at her throat as her head tilted back and she relished in the sensation of his tongue sliding up the inside of her thigh.

The way she writhed beneath his touch, giving herself over to him completely and unabashedly...it unleashed something within him. It was more than just sex. More than two people coming together to quench the need their bodies had conjured up and couldn't relinquish. The connection he'd found with Camilla—the one he felt the moment he opened the door a few days ago and first laid eyes on her—was more than physical. It went beyond that, deeper, sending his body into overdrive, yes, but also consuming his mind, too, keeping thoughts of her at the forefront of his mind at all times. Even the most inopportune ones.

But it led him there. To that room, where the darkness that surrounded them was only marred by the glow of the pale moon shining through his bedroom window, letting him take in her creamy bare flesh and the molten desire in her eyes. Letting him know she felt the same way.

She watched him intently, her chest heaving with each breath as Brock peeled away her panties and crawled his way up her body to lift her and unclasp her bra.

"You're so fucking beautiful." His eyes skimmed every inch of her naked body as he pulled the clothes away from her and tossed them to the floor. At the edge of the bed, he freed himself of his boxer briefs and stood before her, doing everything in his power to calm himself, to remind himself that he should take it slow, be gentle and enjoy the moment.

The bigger part of him, though, the part that ached and throbbed with the need to show her just how many ways there were to be his, was in control. He was sure that streak of dominance was alight in his gaze.

"Camilla..." Brock wasn't sure what he was going to say. A warning? An apology?

"It's okay, Brock." She silenced him with those two words, and she ruined every chance she had at a gentle lovemaking when she coyly opened her thighs, inviting him in.

Their mouths suddenly crashed together again, and he had no recollection of kneeling back down onto the bed. He was on her, like a wild animal with his prey caught between his hands, and the thick head of his erection pressed firmly against her warm folds. He ground his thickness against her, all too aware of the wetness there, too aware of the hardness of her nipples against his chest and the desperate breaths that she gasped each time he rocked his hips against her.

"Please..." she pleaded with him. "Oh God, please."

Listening to her beg...that almost made him come undone. One of his hands came between them and he guided his rigid length more firmly against her entrance. A hard thrust had him inside her to the hilt, and they both gasped against each other's mouths, overcome by the sensations that coursed through their bodies.

Inside her like that, Brock let his instincts take over. He succumbed to his need to be the one to drive her into euphoric bliss, and his hips began to move, kissing her hard and passionately while his hardness filled her so perfectly that he was sure his body was custom-made for hers alone.

Every slam of his hips against hers was a feverish stroke meant to make her succumb to his power over her. He was determined to make her shatter beneath him. His lips pressed against hers, devouring her whimpers and incessant moans, her breath coming out in shallow pants each time his cock was driven back into her to the hilt.

Camilla's hips bucked to meet his, and a wave of dark satisfaction rolled through Brock knowing she was so willing to take everything he gave her. It fuelled his increased pace, and he drove every inch of his shaft into her relentlessly.

Her whimpers were lost amidst their kiss, and he refused to let up. Camilla's hands rounded his lower back and crept to his ass, squeezing his cheeks and forcing him down onto her harder, faster.

This time, he was the one fighting back a fucking whimper. The beautiful woman wanted *more*. The intoxicating sensation of pleasure and pain as he thrust into her with hard, forceful strokes wasn't enough.

Maybe it would never be enough.

His furious rhythm became a frenzy of long, deliberate strokes, bucking his hips to meet hers and slamming her back into the mattress.

Camilla whispered, "Oh God...oh God, yes..." in labored breaths, writhing beneath Brock and digging her fingernails into his shoulder blades, a sting that only stoked the fire that was fueling his relentless thrusts.

"You're mine, Camilla," he grunted out, his gaze blazing with the truth of his words. "You're mine." He could feel the tightening of her core around his thick hardness, squeezing him and violently coaxing him closer to the edge of his release.

"I am." No hesitation on her part. Nothing but submission and desire to be exactly that.

Her confession broke the last shred of his resolve, and his release raged through him, hard and fast. A low, guttural growl escaped his lips as he slammed into her tight channel unabashedly, desperate to deliver those last few thrusts that would send her careening over the cliff with him.

The sharp gasp that tumbled from her lips announced Camilla's orgasm, and Brock had just enough wherewithal to clamp his large hand over her mouth before she screamed out his name and let her release crash through her body like a tidal wave. The tightening and clenching of her muscles, mixed with the throbbing and twitching of his erection, collided and then ebbed together, reducing them both to a series of sporadic shudders and tangled limbs.

"That was incredible," Camilla sighed once her breathing started to even out. "You're incredible."

A playful smirk played on Brock's mouth. "And you're mine."

She grinned at him lazily. "So, you did hear that confession, huh?"

"Oh, I heard it." He leaned over and kissed her mouth, just hard enough to steal the breath away that she thought she'd regained. "And I'm going to hold you to it."

CHAPTER
SIX
BROCK

Brock had never been so reluctant to leave his house and head to the university the next morning. Not only had he had a very long, very sexy night with Camilla, but he found himself cringing at the thought of having to leave her there to take care of Rynn without him while he taught his morning class. Of course, it had to be a day where he taught two classes, one in the morning and one in the afternoon as well.

That only made him groan louder.

Brock loved his job as a professor, and he loved being able to teach his students about the greats amongst the world of English literature.

He found out last night that he also loved having Camilla under him, too. Under his body, under his tongue, everything.

But he was the one that was under her spell. Camilla captivated him like no other. There was no other reason he would have spent the previous day aching for her, having to rush home and take her the way he did. He hadn't felt that kind of intimate pull from someone else in a long time.

He recognized it, though. And he couldn't wait to re-enact

last night's steamy antics again tonight. Which was exactly why he didn't want to leave the house that morning—he didn't want to have to wait to have her again.

But, once again, they had to be responsible adults. He also wasn't sure how to explain it to Rynn just yet, or if it was too soon to try to do that. Camilla was just as willing to make his daughter believe she'd arrived early, before Rynn had gotten out of bed, and they'd been careful to make sure the little girl hadn't seen Camilla come out of Brock's bedroom.

His classes at the university went by at a snail's pace. He followed the curriculum set out for him, and he answered questions from the class both efficiently and expertly, but every time he let his eyes lower to the screensaver on his cellphone which showed a clock, he had to stifle the groan that threatened to bubble up in his throat.

The waiting was excruciating. His body was already buzzing with the wanting Camilla had left him with that morning, the desire that coursed through him and seared his veins from the tips of his fingers to the tips of his toes. The throbbing of his dick only seemed to escalate as flashes of vivid mental images from the night before attacked his mind.

A snapshot of Camilla's splayed thighs. An audible clip of her moaning out his name desperately that sounded so real he was sure other people heard it, too. The ghost of sensual pressure on his lips, like he could still feel the warmth of hers as they melded together in passionate perfection.

Good God, he had to get the hell home to her as soon as he could.

By the time he made it through the front door of his house, he was so turned on by the intoxicating thoughts of Camilla that plagued his mind that he half-hoped Rynn had fallen asleep early, just so he could alleviate some of the intense desire that was causing his balls to ache so damn bad.

Half-hoped. He had spent the entire day away from his daughter, and those were the days that his heart ached to see her once five o'clock rolled around. Nothing could beat hearing an exuberant four-year-old jabber on about her day, even if that day was filled with mostly imaginary things she'd played and games that included faraway castles and other make-believe creatures and people.

He could hear his daughter tittering about a prince and his white horse, telling someone to just wait because he would be there soon to save her from the evil queen. At least, that was what he thought she said. Sometimes, it was hard to tell with her jumbled words and slight lisp.

The one thing he could tell for sure was that Rynn wasn't talking to Camilla. He could hear Camilla's voice coming from the opposite direction. She was in the kitchen, he thought. A smile erupted on Brock's lips when he mused that Camilla's incessant jabbering sounded a lot like Rynn's, only she wasn't discussing princes on white horses or castles. There was also no mistaking that Camilla had prepared an amazing meal. The mix of delicious scents wafting out from the kitchen couldn't be bought from a takeout place.

He kicked off his shoes and padded his way across the floor into the kitchen doorway. He wasn't trying to be quiet, but obviously Camilla didn't hear him. Her back was to him as she paced slowly near the patio door, her cellphone tucked against her ear. Her hands waved expressively as she spoke, something Brock noticed she did quite frequently.

"It's temporary, sweetie," she said, sounding exasperated. "It won't last."

Whatever the person on the other end of the phone said, it made Camilla shake her head vehemently despite the fact that no one could see her.

Well, she *thought* no one could see her.

Brock stood motionless, his breath caught in his throat and his hands tightening into clenched fists at his sides. Surely, she couldn't be talking about him. Or *them*, as he would articulate it, as there had definitely been a union between them last night between his bedsheets. It wasn't about him, or her. It was about them.

"It's okay," Camilla continued, trying to reassure whomever she was having the conversation with. "Trust me, I know what I'm doing."

At that moment, Brock could have used a little reassurance of his own. But he had heard everything he needed to hear. He knew everything he needed to know.

This, him and her, was a temporary thing. She didn't plan on staying on as Rynn's caregiver, and she certainly didn't plan on allowing Brock to be anything more to her than a casual fuck.

He suddenly felt like a complete idiot for having believed it *was* more than casual.

You knew better, he reminded himself. *And yet, you let her get to you.*

That was the part that irked him most. He didn't let her do anything. There had been no conscious thought or decision to take things to the next level with Camilla. It had happened effortlessly. Naturally.

That was why Brock had felt that maybe she was the one.

And she was. The one that was going to screw him over, that is. The woman was just playing games, using Rynn as a paycheck and using him as a way to let off some pent-up steam. Funny, suddenly the only visions running through his head were the ones showing what it would be like to punch his hand through the wall to alleviate some of his frustration and hurt.

Camilla ended the call and was just tucking the phone back into her pocket when she turned around to see him standing there. Her face brightened into a wide smile. "Hey, you. I didn't hear you come in." She closed the gap between them. "How are things?"

He couldn't bring himself not to notice the way she wet her bottom lip with her tongue, or the way her eyes danced with the innuendo of what the evening would bring.

Could have brought.

"Clearer," Brock replied, defeated. "Much clearer."

CHAPTER **SEVEN**
CAMILLA

She wasn't sure what happened.

Waking up to Brock, with decadent recollections of the night before still running rampant through her mind, was heavenly. In the early morning light, he had held her close, her head resting comfortably on his chest as he spoke softly about the classes he had to teach that day and the staff meeting that was occurring in between those classes. She promised a dinner would be ready for him by the time he got home—and she planned to outdo herself, wanting to impress him with her cooking skills—and relished in the crooked smile that notion managed to bring to his face.

They sounded comfortable with each other. Like they were something more than just the nanny and the professor, or the single daddy and the hired help.

She wanted to be more. Hell, last night there was no way she could have thought they were anything less than more.

Because of that, she had gone over and above her duties of being only a nanny to Rynn and she'd made it her mission for the day to look after Brock, too, making sure he had a decent home-cooked meal to come home to at the end of a long work day. Rynn had even helped to scoop the carrots and celery into the pot, and they had made a fun game out of kneading biscuit dough and cutting it into shapes.

It warmed her heart to see the little girl so excited to help her, so much so that even Camilla had fun putting that much work and effort into such a complex dinner menu. Usually, she reserved her fancy dinner ideas for holidays and special occasions.

Today, she figured that making dinner for someone who managed to capture her heart was a special occasion.

She had the roast in the oven and had pulled the plates and cutlery from the cupboards and drawers, intent on setting the table up elaborately to give it that special occasion kind of feel, when her cellphone rang in her pocket. Rynn had gotten bored with the mundane chopping and cutting that she wasn't allowed to help with, so she'd meandered back into the living room to watch *101 Dalmations* for the gazillionth time, and play with her dolls and plastic castle.

Upon answering the phone, Camilla immediately wished she hadn't. She wasn't in the frame of mind to handle her best friend's theatrics went it came to her upcoming wedding, but she knew as soon as she saw her name on the caller display that that was exactly what Shannah was going to vent to her —theatrics. Lots and lots of them.

Sure enough, Shannah was convinced for the hundredth time since her engagement that Paul, her fiancé, was intent on ending the engagement. Why else would he be so nonchalant about the color of the ribbons on the bouquets and the shape of the doilies that the centerpieces sat on in the middle of each table at the reception?

It was on the tip of Camilla's tongue to be blunt and honest—because Paul was a guy. Because men, for the most part, didn't give a damn about stuff like that. Hell, some women didn't care about that stuff, either. But Shannah did, and Camilla, as her maid of honor, had to be respectful of that. So, she had done everything in her power to try to talk her friend off a ledge. Shannah, however, was particularly distraught over her and Paul's most recent argument about these little things, convinced he wasn't going to forgive her this time.

"It's temporary, sweetie," she told her as matter-of-factly as she could. "It won't last."

Once she finally got Shannah calmed down enough on that topic, the bride-to-be promptly switched topics, determined to find out something, anything, about the surprise bridal shower that Camilla and the three bridesmaids were putting on for her in a few weeks' time. That was one thing that Camilla wasn't going to budge on, though. She'd made it this far to keep the bridal shower details a surprise, and be damned if she was going to spill the beans about it now.

"It's okay," she laughed when Shannah tried to tell her it wasn't natural for the bride not to know what was happening in regard to her own wedding. "Trust me, I know what I'm doing."

She didn't feel like she had a clue what she was doing, but the sentiment seemed to ease Shannah's mind and that was all that mattered.

She'd been relieved to end the call, and the sight of Brock standing in the doorway had only added to her elation.

Like a moth to a flame she had gone to him, closed the gap between them because she felt compelled to be closer to him, even if they never truly touched.

And they didn't. She asked him about his day, which gleaned an odd answer.

"How are things?"

"Clearer," he'd said flatly. "Much clearer."

She wanted to question him, ask for clarification. Brock didn't give her the chance. Something had changed in his expression. There was a darkness in his eyes, but it wasn't the broody, mischievous darkness she had witnessed the night before in his bedroom. There was something different in his piercing gaze.

"Are you okay, Brock?"

Camilla reached out to touch his arm, but he bypassed her completely and set his briefcase up on the counter. There was no way he could have missed the stack of plates on the countertop, ready to be placed around the table, no way he couldn't have smelled the delicious aroma of the roast from the oven. And yet, he turned around, his eyes blazing as they locked on her.

"Never better, Camilla." His throat moved visibly. "But I have a lot of work to get done tonight. As for Rynn, I can take it from here."

She was being...dismissed.

"Brock, if there's something wrong—"

"As I just said—" He cut her off, his voice raising an octave. Not a shout, but definitely showing off his assertive stance. "I've got a busy night ahead of me. Thanks for your help today." Almost as an afterthought, he added, "And Rynn's going to spend tomorrow with my mother, so your services won't be needed."

My services. It was like last night hadn't even happened. She was just the nanny, not the woman he'd called beautiful while he owned her body in the darkness of his bedroom.

"Okay." Camilla didn't know what to say. She was dumbfounded, completely taken aback. And the worst part, she thought, as she slipped on her shoes and tugged her purse up onto her shoulder as she headed out the door, was that she didn't have a clue what she had done wrong.

CHAPTER **EIGHT**
BROCK

Brock was distracted again, but this time, for a different reason.

He felt foolish. More than that, he felt utterly ridiculous for ever thinking that fucking his kid's nanny was a good idea. For ever thinking that the nanny wasn't just the nanny at all, but that she was the one.

His one.

Brock had let his loneliness and his primal urges get the best of him. He'd obviously read all the signals wrong, and he'd obviously been very, very wrong about Camilla Benton.

It's temporary. It won't last.

"You got that right," he muttered under his breath. But the only reason his time with Camilla was temporary or short-lived was because she made it that way. He just couldn't figure out how he had been so blindsided by her, how he didn't see it coming.

The truth was, he'd been just as willing to jump into bed with her and ignore what was so blatant—they'd moved too fast, and in the blur of those movements Brock had misread Camilla's intentions.

Brock wondered if Camilla had meant for him to misread

the signals she sent. But that thought hurt him more than the rest of it combined, so he tried hard not to let it surface into the forefront of his mind.

Unfortunately, he wasn't doing a very good job of controlling his thoughts at all.

In his office at the university, he spent the time he should have been grading essays and prepping for his upcoming class that evening instead replaying his night with Camilla over and over in his head, quickly and cruelly followed by the words she'd told whomever was on the phone with her yesterday afternoon. He'd spent the previous evening in a daze, feeling like hell for being so cold and distant with Camilla, and for letting her leave the way he did.

But what did she expect? He had a four-year-old daughter he had to put first, and he wasn't into playing games and one-night stands. He was a single father, and he had to be a protective, responsible one.

A soft knock on his office door snapped Brock from his spiraling thoughts. It was hardly an interruption when he wasn't getting any closer to a resolution, anyway.

"Come in."

If he hadn't already been sitting, someone could have knocked him over with a feather at the sight of Camilla in the doorway.

"Camilla." Brock couldn't stop himself from letting her name fall from his lips, his genuine surprise evident. He stood, though he didn't know what for. "What are you doing here?"

"The liaison office downstairs told me where to find your office." She didn't come into the room any further. "I want to talk to you. About yesterday."

Brock looked down at the pile of essays to his right, then to the opened one in front of him. "I'm really kind of busy right—"

"What happened?" she interjected. Camilla's eyes were wide and shrouded in confusion.

"Nothing," Brock replied. "I just—"

"You just dismissed me, like the night before didn't happen," she insisted. "Like what you and I did together didn't matter. Then, you arranged for Rynn to go to your mom's? That was a low blow, Brock, especially when I don't know what the hell is going on."

"You're a fine one to talk about low blows," he snapped. A loud sigh fled his mouth and he raked a hand through his hair. "Come inside and close the door, will you?" The last thing he needed was the rest of the faculty hearing about his extracurricular activities with the nanny and his misguided attempt at a relationship.

Camilla stepped into the office and closed the door, then she whirled around, probably intent on ripping into him, but Brock had rounded his desk to make sure the door was, indeed, shut, and, judging by the wideness of her eyes, he was closer to her than she expected.

"What do you mean by that?" If her words were meant to be strong and assertive, they were lacking in both.

Brock felt as though he was hanging on by a thread. First, she had the audacity to screw him over the way she did, then she tracked him down at the university—at his place of employment, where he was respected and where he kept a lid on his personal life—to rehash the juicy demise of the relationship they'd barely begun? The relationship that she planned to end in the first place once she got whatever it was she wanted from him?

"Is the problem that I ended whatever was going on between us before you got the chance to? Is that what this is about?" There was an edge to Brock's voice, but he couldn't deny, he was genuinely curious.

"The problem is that it ended at all, Brock." The mix of exasperation and hurt in her voice had him immediately rethinking his choice of words, making his gut twist tightly. "I want to know *why* you ended it, though," she added. "I want to know why you ended us before we even had a chance to see where it would go."

Brock let out a hollow scoff. She had a lot of gall, that was for sure. "You know what, Camilla? You can play your little games with me, but don't you dare play games when it comes to my daughter." He held up a finger. "On second thought, don't bother playing them with me, either. It's not my thing."

Camilla's eyes narrowed, her mouth opening and closing. If she was at a loss for words, Brock sure as hell wasn't.

"I heard your phone conversation," he blurted out. "Rynn and I aren't going to be someone's temporary anything. You seemed pretty confident yesterday that you and I weren't going *to last—*" He made quotation marks with his fingers. "—so I went ahead and made sure of it, before anything went any further."

She stared at him, bewildered. Then, Brock watched as all the pieces seemed to fall into place and Camilla finally understood what he was saying. "Wait, that's what this is all about?"

"Yeah, that's exactly what this is all about." Like her, he wanted to sound damn sure of himself. Except, he wasn't feeling that sure at all, purely because Camilla's reaction wasn't at all what he expected, and she suddenly didn't look nearly as distraught as she'd been when she first showed up.

Camilla took a step forward and shoved her purse onto his desk, zipping it open to fish through it. When she found what she was looking for, she pulled it out. A rectangular piece of cardstock was between her fingers, pale yellow in color with gold foil calligraphy on one side. "Actually, *that's* exactly what this is about." She shoved the card toward him, forcing him to take it.

Brock turned the card in his hands. It was a wedding invitation with the image of a sunflower on it. He held it up to her. "What the hell does this have to do with anything?"

"Everything!" Camilla exclaimed. "You only heard my side of the conversation, Brock, and you just chose to hear what you wanted to hear. When I mentioned things being temporary and that they wouldn't last, I was talking about my friend, Shannah, and her fiancé. They're arguing about their damn wedding again, and it's my duty as her maid of honor to calm her down. Obviously, my words did little to calm you down, however."

Brock stared at the yellow invitation, then up at Camilla's face, and back again. All the air had been sucked from the room. "So, you weren't talking about us."

"I never even mentioned you in that conversation, Brock. She never let me get a word in about anything other than the wedding and the bridal shower." She reached out for the invitation. "I'm not playing games with you and Rynn," she added, her voice softer. "And I sure as hell had no intentions of ending *this*, you and I, before it even got started."

Brock grabbed her by the arm she had extended and he pulled her to him. His lips crashed against hers, and he kissed her with every ounce of apology and pain and passion that warred within him.

"I'm so fucking sorry," he panted out, his lips still grazing against hers as he clutched her against him.

Camilla's chest heaved as well, and it wasn't until Brock held her close that he realized she was trembling with the emotion she struggled to keep at bay.

"It's okay," she whispered, her eyes heavy-lidded and ignited with the turmoil he'd caused her. "Make it up to me."

Brock guided her backward until her thighs met the edge of his desk. He'd never been so happy for her to wear a skirt. His mouth trailed from her lips, down the side of her throat where he could feel the wild pulsing just beneath her skin, to her collarbone, where he sucked and nipped at her tender flesh as he worked at hiking her skirt up her thighs and pushing her up onto the edge of his desk.

Camilla fumbled with the silver buckle of his belt while he pushed her skirt as far as he could out of his way and scrambled to push her silky panties to the side. She let out a startled, lust-laden gasp when he pressed one long finger up inside her, stroking her slick walls and basking in the hot wetness that was caused by her desire for him.

"Fuck, Camilla…" He slowly moved his thick digit in and out, biting down on her collarbone as she rubbed at his rock-solid length through his pants. "Fuck, baby, yes."

Keeping his finger inside her, he used his other hand to help her get his belt and pants undone and pushed out of the way. He needed her, craved her. And he was desperate to prove to her he was sorry for his stupidity.

Camilla, in a frenzy, pushed his pants and boxer briefs down his thighs and let his rigid hardness spring free. Her wetness, his hardness…they were desperate for each other.

Brock withdrew his finger and stepped in closer between her thighs. He didn't wait—he couldn't bear to—and he pushed his solid length into her soft, soaked core in one powerful thrust.

Camilla cried out, but the sound was lost somewhere amidst her mouth and his. He kissed her hard and intensely, swallowing the feverish sounds of their relentless plight towards bliss, gripping her hips tightly and guiding her against him to meet each incessant thrust.

Again and again, he pulled out just to the tip, then slammed into her again, relishing in the intoxicating sounds that vibrated off her tongue onto his.

Camilla clutched his shoulders for dear life, clinging to him and taking every solid clash of their hips with the intimate determination of a woman being fueled by her physical desires and her emotional needs.

She'd begged for him to make it up to her, and she was letting him. Giving herself over to him.

Submitting to him and his apologies and his unabashed craving to have her as his own.

It was hard and it was fast, but the moment when they both careened over the edge and found their release together, it was cleansing as well. They'd found their common ground again, reminded themselves of the connection that held them together as though attached by a tether, and felt the relentless heat and ache and tingle that came with being completely and utterly consumed by someone.

By each other.

They couldn't take back what had happened due to their miscommunication, but Brock knew he would spend the rest of his life trying to make up for his mistakes. Not because Camilla asked him to, but because he wanted to.

Because he wanted *her*, and there was no way he could deny that now.

EPILOGUE
CAMILLA

Shannah's wedding went off without a hitch. Despite her continuous worries about the state of her and Paul's relationship and the incessant nitpicking of all the little things regarding her wedding day, Shannah and Paul were married on a sunny autumn day, and neither of them had ever looked happier.

Camilla felt like she could finally breathe a sigh of relief. She had taken her maid of honor duties seriously, and every responsibility that had landed on her was fulfilled, and fulfilled well. She could finally enjoy the party, just like everyone else.

It had been almost three months since her misunderstanding with Brock. And to think, if she'd never gone to his office at the university that day, they might never have had the fairy-tale relationship they did now.

She still stayed with Rynn every day while Brock went to the university, but Camilla had her name removed from the nanny agency. She had no intentions of seeking other jobs in the field, and she didn't think it was right to stay listed as such when that's not at all what she was anymore.

Rynn knew that Camilla and Brock were a couple now, as

much as a four-year-old girl could understand. Thankfully, she'd never broached the subject of her being her mommy while Brock was away at the university. It wasn't that she didn't want to fill the role of the girl's mother, but Camilla didn't want to have to tackle that specific question without the support of Brock at her side.

But they'd been content with the little family they'd become, figuring out each other's little quirks and becoming acquainted with sharing their lives together.

Camilla still lived in her own apartment, though. She was just as adamant as Brock about keeping things as normal and easy for Rynn as possible. While there were many nights that she stayed over long after Brock's daughter fell asleep, and there were many mornings where Camilla was miraculously there before Rynn's sleepy head got out of bed, she and Brock had been very careful to maintain that level of separation in front of his daughter. Other than the occasional kiss and holding hands, they kept their romantic life private and away from prying eyes.

Shannah, however, was ecstatic that her maid of honor was bringing a date to the wedding. Camilla wasn't sure whether to laugh at her friend's surprise or be a little insulted that it was such a big deal, but either way, Shannah and Paul seemed to hit it off with Brock from the first introduction, so that was another huge relief in Camilla's favor.

He seemed to stay on the sidelines throughout the ceremony. Camilla couldn't blame him. Brock didn't know anyone there but her. But as she stood at the front of the church while her friends repeated their vows and became husband and wife, she managed to glance over at him and catch his gaze. Brock's eyes were locked on hers, and the smile that crept across his face made her blush.

He'd been watching her, no one else. She was sure of it.

At the reception at the community center, all duties finally done, Camilla sought him out. She found him near the punch bowl just as the hor d'oeuvres were being brought out and the music began to play from the strategically placed speakers.

"You look mighty strapping in that suit, Mr. Hanlin."

He turned at the sound of her voice, mischief already in his eyes. "That mister stuff is reserved for students and law enforcement. Wait, are you a cop?" He reached out and pulled her closer to him. "Have I been a bad, bad boy?"

Camilla laughed. "Guess we'll find out later, won't we?"

"That's a guarantee, Cam."

She loved it that he'd taken to calling her Cam, just like Rynn did. It was endearing, and just a little bit sexy to hear it on his lips, said in such an intimate manner. "Are you having fun?"

"I'm having fun watching you." He grinned, taking a sip of the punch he'd poured in a plastic cup. "You look absolutely breathtaking. I don't think I've told you that enough tonight."

She blushed. "You've told me about a hundred times, but thank you."

The song track changed, switching from a fast-paced dance song to something slower and more geared towards tender touches and slow swaying.

"Dance with me."

Camilla was surprised by Brock's demand. He had never seemed like the type to be much of a dancer before. But be damned if she was going to turn him down.

"I'd love to."

He took her by the hand and guided her out onto the dancefloor amongst the other paired couples that were there. She became acutely aware of the heat of his hand at the small of her back and the dampness of his breath on her cheek as he held her close, expertly leading her around the dancefloor like he'd done it a million times before.

"You're quite the dancer," she whispered in his ear, kissing his lobe gently.

"My mother taught me when I was young," he explained. "Said it was a requirement if I wanted to be a gentleman when I grew up."

"And is that what you are?" She chuckled. "A complete gentleman?"

"Only when it counts, baby." He pulled back and gave her a cocky grin that left her core aching with the sweet promise of the night they would share together. "I might be quite the dancer, but you're quite the ravishing beauty tonight, Cam. I mean it. You're that, as well as a lot of other things."

She practically purred in his ear. She couldn't help it. His sweet words were like an aphrodisiac. By the time they did manage to make it out of there, she was going to be raring to rip his clothes off. "Mmm, and what else am I, baby?"

Brock twirled her around. "You're gorgeous."

He kissed her neck. "You're absolutely amazing with Rynn Tin Tin."

He nipped at her sensitive flesh just enough to get her attention and heighten the arousal that was burning up her veins. "And you're mine."

She whimpered a sound meant to convey that she agreed, but Brock pulled away, staring into her eyes. She could see the twinkling lights that surrounded them reflecting back at her in his eyes. There was something else in his stare, too. "What is it?" she asked, a hint of worry in her tone.

"That's a lie, isn't it?"

"What?" Their perfect arcs and smooth movements as they danced to the song had ceased.

"You're not mine in every way," he said. "Not every way that counts to me, anyway."

"Brock, I don't know what you're saying," she whispered to him, alarmed. "Of course, I am. I—"

"So, I want to change that," he interjected. He let go of her waist long enough to retrieve a small crimson box from his jacket pocket. "I want to make you mine in every way that counts, Camilla."

She stood there, her hands hanging on to him loosely, as much for support as anything, in complete awe, as Brock opened the little box and revealed a white gold filigree band with three diamonds in it. "I know that the three-stoned diamond rings are supposed to represent past, present, and future, but I saw this ring and thought of you, me, and Rynn." He reached up and brushed away a tear that had escaped onto her cheek. "I want the three of us to be a family, Camilla. Will you marry me?"

She broke into a fit of sobs, her hands covering her mouth as she emphatically nodded her head yes, over and over, because she couldn't seem to get the word out.

"I take it that's a yes?" Brock chuckled.

She playfully swatted at him. "Definitely a yes," she choked out. "Yes."

Brock wore the widest grin as he plucked the ring from the box and slipped it onto her finger, then he wrapped her in the tightest hug, clutching her against his chest like a lifeline. She couldn't speak, and when she felt his lips touch against her ear, she thought he was going to say something else that would make her happy tears continued to stream down her face.

"I know you're anticipating tonight," he whispered. There was no mistaking the deviousness in his tone. "Just the two of us. Believe me, I am, too. Just wait, my beautiful fiancée, because I plan on making you the happiest woman on the planet."

"In what way?" she asked him coyly.

"In *every* way."

Camilla knew two things for sure. The first was that there was no way to misinterpret that. The second was that she couldn't wait to do a little celebrating of her own with him. Just the two of them.

ABOUT THE AUTHOR

Cass Kincaid writes steamy romance stories, creates HEAs, and loves every damn minute of it. She LOVES love, and she's a hopeless romantic. Oh, and she has a thing for sexy, sarcastic fictional boyfriends, but don't we all?

ABOUT THE PUBLISHER

EverLust Books is an imprint of Harbor Lane Books, LLC. We are a US-based independent digital publisher of steamy contemporary romance to erotic fiction.

Connect with EverLust Books on our website www.everlustbooks.com and TikTok, Instagram, and Twitter @everlustbooks.

ALSO BY CASS KINCAID

www.ingramcontent.com/pod-product-compliance
Lightning Source LLC
LaVergne TN
LVHW092059060526
838201LV00047B/1469